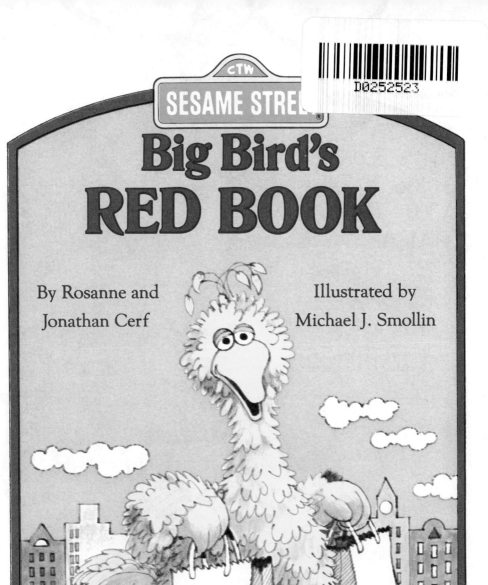

SESAME STREET

Big Bird's
RED BOOK

By Rosanne and
Jonathan Cerf

Illustrated by
Michael J. Smollin

A SESAME STREET/GOLDEN PRESS BOOK

Published by Western Publishing Company, Inc.,
in conjunction with Children's Television Workshop.

© 1990, 1977 Children's Television Workshop. Sesame Street puppet characters © 1990 Jim Henson Productions, Inc. All rights reserved. Printed in the U.S.A. No part of this book may be reproduced or copied in any form without written permission from the publisher. Sesame Street and the Sesame Street sign are registered trademarks and service marks of Children's Television Workshop. All other trademarks are the property of Western Publishing Company, Inc. ISBN: 0-307-01029-5   MCMXCI

This educational book was created in conjunction with the Children's Television Workshop, producers of Sesame Street. Children do not have to watch the television show to benefit from this book. Workshop revenues from this product will be used to support CTW educational projects.